200_

To Lauren -
Happy Birthday.

Love,
Aunt
Denise

Everybody Moos At Cows!

Even Matthew McFarland

Lisa Funari Willever

Illustrations by
Elaine Poller
and
Glenn Byrne

Special Guest Young Author & Illustrator Section

We Support

**Children of
the World**

Franklin Mason Press

Trenton, New Jersey

To my parents, Lorraine & Rennie, and all parents who refuse to give into the whining, moaning, and groaning! Also, for Anthony and Paula, my childhood car-mates – "Mooooo"….**LFW**

To "The Girls"- Mom, Lisa, and little Sarah! Thanks for all of your love and support……**EP**

To my father, a continuing source of inspiration. I love you, Dad…..**GB**

The editors of Franklin Mason Press would like to offer their gratitude to those who have contributed their time and energy to this project: Mr. Reynold Funari, Ms. Lorraine Funari, Ms. Rebecca Matthias, Mr. Dan Matthias, Mr. Priit Pals, Ms. Karen Pals, Mr. Donald Greenwood, Mr. Robert Quackenbush, Ms. Karen Aiello, Ms. Geraldine Willever, Mr. Brian Hughes, Ms. Adrienne Supino, Ms. Wanda Bowman, Ms. Nancy Volpe, Ms. Stacey Williams, Ms. Dawn Hiltner, and all of our friends at the New Jersey Education Association and the National Education Association.

Also, a special thanks to those who have worked tirelessly on the Guest Young Author & Illustrator Committees. Your care in selecting the work of young authors and artists will help to shape and inspire the writers and illustrators of tomorrow.

Cover and Interior Design by Peri Poloni, Knockout Design, Cameron Park, CA
www.knockoutbooks.com

Published in the United States. Printed in Singapore.
Franklin Mason Press ISBN 0-9679227-0-4
Library of Congress Control Number: 2001090624

Children of
the World

Franklin Mason Press is proud to support the important work of Children of the World Adoptions.
In that spirit, $0.25 will be donated from the sale of each book.

A fter lunch, the kids all meet from every house on Franklin Street. With balls and bikes and bats they play. This is how they spend their day.

But Sunday never turns out good.

It never works out like it should.

The other kids are all outside,

while I'm preparing for **"The Ride!"**

Home is where
I'd rather stay,
outside with
all my friends
and play.

Time is ticking,
I need a plan.
I must outsmart the
"FAMILY MAN!"

SLUGGER

TICK-TOCK!
TICK-TOCK!
TICK-TOCK!

I'd say my chores

have been neglected

or tell him that I am infected.

Even though each time I've tried,

I always end up on the ride.

So now I'll make my final plea, "Can you take the ride, but not take me?"

Of course the answer's always, "No, it's family time and **YOU WILL GO!**"

A family of five piled into the car,

to places never near but far.

And as I wave to each playmate,

I swear I won't cooperate.

When he says, "Matt, look at the farms." I'll turn my head and fold my arms.

When he says, "Matt, enjoy the view." I'll close my eyes, that's what I'll do.

When he pulls up along some sheep, I'll make believe I am asleep.

And every time he says a word, I'll just pretend I haven't heard.

There's a farm ahead, he will not pass. Cows are grazing in the grass.

He stops the car and starts to "Moo"...the cows, they don't know what to do.

If cows could talk, they'd surely say, "Someone should put this man away."

And when I've taken all I can...my family joins the Family Man!

First my sister, then my brother,

and last we have my mooing mother!

Each "moo" is meant to be the best

and each one moos to beat the rest.

But there's no way

you'll hear me **MOOING,**

that's one thing I won't be doing.

I'd rather wear a monkey suit...

with a four foot hat

that's made of fruit.

Finally, I'm glad to say, he starts the car, we're on our way.

But this is more than I can take,
instead of home...we're at the lake!

We're here to feed the ducks and geese. They line up for a stale bread feast.

ith each one looking for a slice, I'm hoping that these geese are nice.

B ut the geese are huge, in fact, they're LARGE,

they see the bread, they start to charge.

I wonder as I hold this bread,

when was the last time they were fed?

They must have thought this was a game, the more I ran...

The more they came. I tried so hard to shake them loose,

A real live game of duck duck goose!

I started running towards the lake, but that would be a big mistake.

The chances I would win are grim, 'cause I forgot that geese could swim

By now I'm scared, a bit perplexed. I'm terrified of what comes next.

The only hope I have, by far, is if I make it to the car.

The problem is, I'm sad to say,

I've run so far, I've lost my way.

I need to find our parking space.

I need the geese to quit this race!

I see the car, I sure am glad. I'm out of bread, these geese are mad.

I run real far, I run some more. I'm in the car, I lock the door.

Please Do Not Feed The Geese!!

We leave the lake, but soon slow down. This time it's for a country town.

As the car comes to a stop, we're at a local ice cream shop.

Although I wish that I were home, it wouldn't hurt to have a cone.

Forget I said, " Enough's enough!" I think I like this family stuff!

And while I wish it wouldn't end, I know next week…*we'll ride again!*

Guest Young Author

First Place – **Kyle Wilcox**   **Age 8**
Benjamin Franklin School
Lawrenceville, New Jersey

Honey of a Bear

One warm fall day a brown bear that lived in the woods wanted some honey. But the bee would not give him any honey. He was very hungry and he was very thirsty. He thought he would never get any honey.

One day the brown bear met a bee. He was sad. The bear said, "Why are you sad?"

"Because I can't make honey."

So the bee said to the brown bear, "Do you want to be friends?"

The brown bear said to the bee, "Can we try to make honey?"

So the bee went to get some nectar. He went to the bee's nest and got a bowl. Then the bee put the nectar in the bowl. The bear stirred the nectar and the bee got a fan and fanned it. Then a mean bee came and stole all of the honey. Now the bee was very sad. They worked for a whole day to make that honey. The bear was sad, too. The bee asked the bear, "Why does the mean bee steal all of the honey?"

The bear said, "I don't know."

That night, the bear sneaked up and took the mean bee's nest. He ran far away and put it in another tree. The bee stayed home and made more honey. When the bear came home, he had honey for breakfast!

Second Place – **Alyssa Galvez**   **Age 9**
Westminster Academy – School #26
Elizabeth, New Jersey

"It's Okay"

Third Place – **Michael DiBalsi**   **Age 9**
Langtree School
Hamilton, New Jersey

"The Absent-Minded Easter Bunny"

Guest Young Illustrator

First Place – **Melanie Hazlett**   Age 6
Peter Muschal School
Yardville, New Jersey

"A Sunny Day On The Farm"

Second Place – **Katherine Churchill**   Age 6
Cranberry Pines School
Medford, New Jersey

"The Zoo"

Third Place – **Collin Kloc**   Age 6
St. Lawrence Catholic School
Indianapolis, Indiana

"The Beast With Blue Stripes"

Would You Like To Be An Author or Illustrator?

Franklin Mason Press is looking for stories and illustrations from children 6-9 years old to appear in our books. We are dedicated to providing children with an avenue into the world of publishing.

If you would like to be our next Guest Young Author or Guest Young Illustrator, read the information below and send us your work.

To be a Guest Young Author:

Send us a 75-200 word story about something strange, funny, or unusual. Stories may be fiction or non-fiction. Be sure to follow the rules below.

To be a Guest Young Illustrator:

Draw a picture using crayons, markers, or colored pencils. Do not write words on your picture and be sure to follow the rules below.

Prizes

1st Place Author / 1st Place Illustrator

$25.00, a framed award, a complimentary book and your work will be published in FMP's newest book.

2nd Place Author / 2nd Place Illustrator

$15.00, a framed award, a complimentary book and the title of your work and your name will be published in FMP's newest book.

3rd Place Author / 3rd Place Illustrator

$10.00, a framed award, a complimentary book and the title of your work and your name will be published in FMP's newest book.

Rules For The Contest

1. Children may enter one category only, either Author or Illustrator.
2. All stories must be typed or written very neatly.
3. All illustrations must be sent in between 2 pieces of cardboard to prevent wrinkling.
4. Name, address, phone number, school, and parent's signature must be on the back of all submissions.
5. All work must be original and completed solely by the child.
6. Franklin Mason Press reserves the right to print submitted material. All work becomes property of FMP and will not be returned. Any work selected is considered a work for hire and FMP will retain all rights.
7. There is no deadline for submissions. FMP will publish children's work in every book published. All submissions are considered for the most current title.
8. All submissions should be sent to:

Youth Submissions Editor
Franklin Mason Press
P. O. Box 3808
Trenton, NJ 08629
www.franklinmason.com

Tips for Young Authors & Illustrators

1. Write and draw about things you enjoy. If you need an idea, think of your family, your friends, or your favorite things to do.

2. Find a nice quiet place where you can write or draw.

3. If you are having trouble making up your story, make a list of ideas that you want to write about. Use your list to get started.

4. If you become stuck in the middle of a story, put it away and go back to it the next day. Sometimes all you need is to take a break or get some rest.

5. Remember, your first draft of a story is never your last draft! Rewrite, rewrite, rewrite….until it's perfect.

6. Share your stories and illustrations with your friends, family, and teachers.

7. If you are between the ages of 6-9 years old, send your work to Franklin Mason Press …Home of the Guest Young Author and Illustrator Contest!

For ideas and activities for Young Authors and Illustrators, visit

www.franklinmason.com

About Franklin Mason Press

Franklin Mason Press was founded in Trenton, New Jersey in September 1999. While our mission is to produce quality children's books, we also provide children with an avenue into the world of publishing. Our Guest Young Author & Illustrator Contest offers children an opportunity to submit their work and possibly become published authors and illustrators. In addition, Franklin Mason Press is proud to support children's charities with donations from book sales. Each new title benefits a different children's charity.

We are pleased to have formed corporate partnerships with The March of Dimes, St. Jude's Research Hospital, The Four Foundation, and Rosie Adoptions. For more information please visit our website at:

www.franklinmason.com

One of Matthew McFarland's Favorite Charities

Matthew McFarland is nine years old and the oldest kid in his family. He doesn't always do as he's told, he doesn't always play fair, and he usually thinks he knows what is best.

Lucky for Matthew, he has a great family. His parents don't give into his moaning and groaning. They make him do his homework and go to bed on time. They make him help around the house and they make sure he knows who is in charge.

Every title published by Franklin Mason Press benefits a different children's charity. Like Matthew, we wish that **every child** had a great family to teach them and to love them. In that spirit, we have selected Children of the World Adoptions to benefit from the sales of *Everybody Moos At Cows – Even Matthew McFarland*! Read below to learn about their exceptional work.

About Children of the World Adoptions

Children of the World is an adoption agency whose work is geared toward serving the best interests of those children whose lives we touch. In existence for over a decade, we pride ourselves on our unwavering dedication to the welfare of all children.

We work to ensure the health of birth mothers, giving babies the best possible start in addition to a loving family. Prenatal care is an extremely important issue for babies and therefore, one of our top priorities. We offer counseling to birth parent(s) and assist them throughout their pregnancy.

To learn more about adoption, visit:

www.childrenoftheworldadoption.com

Children of the World

ROSIE ADOPTIONS,
the Outreach Division of Children of the World,
can be reached at 1-800-841-0804.

Lisa Funari Willever (author) is a lifelong resident of Trenton, New Jersey and a fourth grade teacher in the Trenton School District. She is a graduate of The College of New Jersey and a member of the National Education Association, the New Jersey Education Association, and the New Jersey Reading Association. She is also the author of *The Culprit Was A Fly, Miracle On Theodore's Street, Maximilian The Great, The Easter Chicken,* and *Chumpkin.* Her husband, Todd is a professional Firefighter in the city of Trenton and the co-author of *Miracle of Theodore's Street.* They are the proud parents of two year old Jessica and one year old Patrick.

Elaine Poller (co-Illustrator) started drawing when she was 3 years old, her first drawings were of a family of characters called "Eekies". Elaine graduated from The College of New Jersey, where she earned a BFA in Graphic Design with a minor in Illustration. Currently, she is a senior designer for a large children's clothing manufacturer in New York City. After too many years of living in a sixth-floor walk-up in Manhattan, she has recently returned home to the Garden State and resides in Edgewater, N.J. with her husband Bradley. This is her first children's book.

Glenn Byrne (co-Illustrator) has always been interested in illustrating childrens books. After graduating fromThe Fashion Institute of Design in New York City, Glenn worked for several companies in New York's famous Garment Center. His talent led him to his current position as a senior artist for a large children's clothing manufacturer. Glenn is a native New Yorker who currently lives in Queens, N.Y. where he spends time rooting for the Yankees with his daughter McKenna, and wife Michele.

Franklin Mason Press

P.O.Box 3808, Trenton, NJ 08629